This book belongs to:

Editor: Alexandra Koken
Designer: Plum Pudding Design

Copyright © QEB Publishing 2012

First published in the United States by
QEB Publishing
3 Wrigley, Suite A
Irvine, CA 92618

A CIP record for this book is available from the Library of Congress.

ISBN 978 1 78171 084 5

Printed in China

Listen Up, Pup!

Steve Smallman and Gill McLean

Toby was a happy dog.
His people were well trained.
They took him for walks...

...tickled his belly...

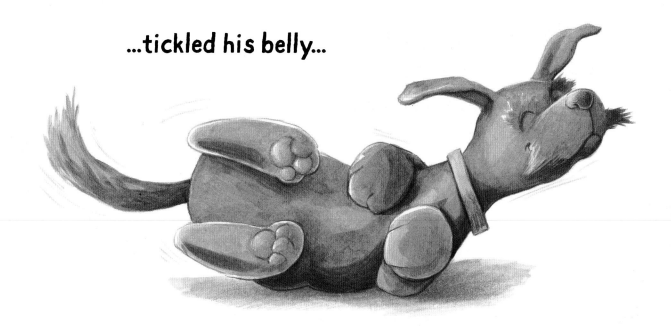

...let him lie on the couch, and, every now and then, gave him a sausage. Yes, life was good.

Until Snoop came along!
Snoop was a cute and fluffy puppy.
Toby didn't like him.

Snoop ran up to Toby, wagging his tail.
Toby barked at Snoop...

...and his people sent Toby to his bed.

"What do they want another dog for?"
Toby grumbled to himself.
"What's the matter with me?"

Toby had a long think about it. Then he sneaked
out of his bed and over to the puppy.
But this time he didn't bark at Snoop...

...he licked him right on the nose!

"Good boy!" cried his people, and they gave him a sausage. "Mmmmm," thought Toby. "Interesting."

"Listen up, pup," said Toby the next day.
"If you're staying, there are a few things you need to learn."

"Lesson one: this is MY bed—stay out of it!"

"Lesson two: this is MY food bowl—stay out of that, too!"

"Lesson three: always make a fuss
about your people when they come home.

You could get a sausage.
But try not to pee on the floor!"

"Lesson four: always let them
know when it's time for a walk...

...they sometimes forget."

"Lesson five: as soon as they take off your leash, run to the pond."

"Can I jump in?"
asked Snoop.

"No, but it's fun to
scare the ducks!"
said Toby.

"Lesson six: you can roll around in poop if you want to—it makes you smell nice!"

"But not everyone thinks so."

"Well done, pup," said Toby. "That's all for now."
"What about chasing?" asked Snoop.

"Chasing?" said Toby. "Well, all right.
You can go first if you like."

And the two dogs chased
each other...

...until they were tired and happy and dizzy.

Toby flopped wearily into his bed.
Snoop forgot all about lesson one and climbed in, too!

But before Toby even had a
chance to complain, his people
scratched his ears and smiled.

"All right, pup," Toby whispered. "You can stay."
And they both fell fast asleep.

Next Steps

Show the children the cover again. Could the children have guessed what the story is about? Read the title together; does that give them a clue?

When the children have read the story, or you have read it to them, ask them why Toby didn't like the puppy at first.

Do the children think Toby liked Snoop at the end of the story?

If so, what made Toby change his mind?

Ask the children if any of them have little brothers or sisters.

Do the children sometimes get a little jealous if Mom or Dad pay a lot of attention to a brother or sister?

Do you think that Toby and Snoop will stay friends even if the sausages run out?

Ask the children to draw a picture of Toby and Snoop.